Willow Come To Tea?

Sylvia Buck

Copyright © 2024 Sylvia Buck

All rights reserved, including the right to reproduce this book, or portions thereof in any form. No part of this text may be reproduced, transmitted, downloaded, decompiled, reverse engineered, or stored, in any form or introduced into any information storage and retrieval system, in any form or by any means, whether electronic or mechanical without the express written permission of the author.

ISBN: 978-1-917425-18-6

Dedication

I would like to dedicate this book to Willow and her family, who inspired me to write this rhyming verse to help raise money for the 'Allergy UK' charity.

Acknowledgement

I would like to say a big thank you to Steph, who has kindly illustrated this book for me. This busy lady not only works full time, but dedicates all of her spare time to the 'Forest Flock Pigeon Sanctuary' charity, so thank you Steph. for helping me out.

Also by this author

The Adventures of Tommy Bones

Willow Come To Tea?

Willow is a little girl
with lots of curly hair.
She loves to sing
and dance and play
but life though isn't fair.

She has some friends at playgroup,
on most days she will see.
One of them asked Willow's mum
if she could come to tea.

'I'm sorry love, but no,'
was Willow's mum's reply.
The little girl was so upset,
in fact it made her cry.

Willow's mum tried very hard
to make the young girl see,
that Willow has a problem
that's called an allergy.

'I'd love her to have tea with you;
I know that would be great.
But certain foods that you can eat
can't go on Willow's plate.'

'Some children can't have eggs or nuts
or fish or milk or bread.
Their parents have to try and find
some other foods instead.'

'These foods can make them poorly
in lots of different ways.
So they must listen carefully
to what the doctor says.'

'Some allergies cause rashes,
their skin might go bright red.
They may be sick or cannot breathe
and have to go to bed.'

'There's lots of different allergies,
some grown-ups have them too.
They just have to be careful
there's not much they can do.'

'I need to watch what Willow eats.
A risk I cannot take.
She may choose something dangerous
and eat it by mistake.'

Willow's friend is satisfied
now that she can see,
the reason little Willow,
cannot come to tea.

Willow

www.ingramcontent.com/pod-product-compliance
Lightning Source LLC
Chambersburg PA
CBHW040242130526
44590CB00049B/4226